Kay Chorao

Little Farm by the Sea

Henry Holt and Company

New York

Henry Holt and Company, Inc., *Publishers since 1866*, 115 West 18th Street, New York, New York 10011

Henry Holt is a registered trademark of Henry Holt and Company, Inc.

Published in Canada by Fitzhenry & Whiteside Ltd., 195 Allstate Parkway, Markham, Ontario L3R 4T8.

Library of Congress Cataloging-in-Publication Data
Chorao, Kay.
Little farm by the sea / Kay Chorao
Summary: Depicts the activities on a small family farm during the four seasons of the year.
[1. Farm life—Fiction.] I. Title.
PZ7.C4463Li 1998 [E]—dc21 97-24431

ISBN 0-8050-5053-1 / First Edition—1998 / Typography by Martha Rago
The artist used gouache and pen and ink on watercolor paper to create the illustrations for this book.
Printed in the United States of America on acid-free paper.∞
1 3 5 7 9 10 8 6 4 2

This book is dedicated to Betty and Garry Brown, who made
Smallholdings Farm such a refuge from urban pressures, providing delicious
organic produce, beautiful flowers, animals for our children to experience,
and, most of all, humor and humanity.

*I*t is still winter.

The little farm by the sea looks asleep. The fields are frozen under early morning frost, and the clamshell driveway is quiet.

Only curious seagulls move through the air.

But inside the barn, life is stirring. Even before the sun
is up, the animals are awake and Farmer Brown's family is
busy. They are milking the cows and feeding warm milk
to the barn cats.

In their stalls, the pigs squeal noisily. They are hungry for their breakfast.

Farmer Brown and his children mix food scraps and vegetables with bread and water. As they fill the feed bowls, the pigs crowd eagerly around. They push and shove and gobble their food.

Farmer Brown goes to the hayloft. He is careful not to disturb a bantam hen who is nesting on one of the steps. He throws down hay for the donkeys and cows. One son helps feed the animals while the other leads the cows from the barn.

The donkeys trot in circles, braying when they see their breakfast.

In their coops behind the barn, the chickens are the last to be fed.

While Farmer Brown fills the feed trays with chicken meal, Mrs. Brown and the children gather eggs.

The hens hop in and out of the nest boxes, leaving perfect brown eggs.

The Browns return to the barn to weigh and sort the eggs.
A scale tells whether an egg goes into a carton marked *Large*
or *Small*. If the eggs are dirty, they are washed in a special
egg washer before they are sorted.

The full cartons are stacked in the selling room.

Soon customers begin to arrive. Sometimes they bring
empty egg cartons for the Browns to use again. They
put the money for their purchases in an old metal box.

When the morning chores are finished, Farmer Brown goes to his machine shop. There he repairs farm machinery and rebuilds antique tractors.

As the days warm, some of the tractors will be seen working in the fields. They may even lead parades or be shown at the County Fair.

A long, pale greenhouse sits near the machine shop. Inside the greenhouse, the air is moist and warm, even on a late winter's day.

Mrs. Brown and her children plant seeds in small plastic cups inside trays known as flats. They label the flats and pots with wooden markers. Every day Mrs. Brown waters the soil and soon bright green seedlings appear.

As the earth warms, Farmer Brown turns the soil with a plow and enriches it with fertilizer from his animals. He plants seeds for green beans, zucchini, beets, broccoli, lettuce, and spinach.

Seedlings are brought from the greenhouse and planted
in the furrowed earth. Everyone helps.
Spring is beginning.

Under a sunny sky, Nettie, Emma, Polly, and Fanny Cow roam.

In the next pasture, geese nibble on grass and weeds. They rush to the fence honk-honking when they see Farmer Brown. He throws them bread scraps.

One little gosling watches Mama Goose drink water. Then she, too, tries drinking from the big pan.

Mama Pig is sleeping in her stall. Soon her summer piglets will be born.

Mama Donkey is eating extra grass, preparing for the birth of her little burro.

Now it is spring! The barn bursts to life. The Browns keep
plenty of flowers, herbs, and vegetables on the porch and in
the selling room.

By the roadside a sign says: "Natural Strawberries You Pick."

Another sign at the barn gives instructions to the strawberry pickers.

Soon young and old are picking juicy strawberries.

Pick your own
1.50 Quart
walk along
pasture to
the lot
watch children
carefully!!
please pay at Barn
10 Quarts or over 1.25

As customers pick, bees buzz around the flowers. The Browns' hives are beginning to fill with honey. Farmer Brown will gather the honey when summer ends and sell it in little plastic-bear jars.

At the roadside stand, customers stop to buy berries, spinach, lettuce, and flowers.

One summer evening, under the moon and stars, Mama Donkey gives birth. Soon the fuzzy burro wobbles to his feet and drinks his mother's milk.

On a summer day, visiting children ask: "Are there piggies yet?"

"Not yet," says Mrs. Brown, smiling.

The children chase Mama Hen and her chicks, who hide in the tall grass.

By the rabbit cage, one of the Brown daughters holds a bunny. Two small children watch.

"Does it bite?" asks the little girl.

Before the older girl can answer "No," the children dash away.

One day, while Farmer Brown
is planting pumpkin seeds in a far
field, visitors find a sign by the barn:
"Quiet Please—Piggies Are Sleeping."
Mama Pig has a litter of piglets
resting beside her.

Each day the piglets grow bigger and livelier.
One piggy finds a gap in the pen. He hops through
and three piglets follow.

They dash through people's legs, upsetting cartons of
beans, berries, eggs, and flowers. At last, they fall asleep
behind a bale of hay.

Full summer is here.

While Mrs. Brown and one of her daughters pick flowers, martins and swallows dart overhead. They eat some of the insects that harm the crops. The martins pop in and out of birdhouses high above the fields and chicken coops. Their favorite houses are gourds grown and dried by Farmer Brown. They swing above the raspberry patch where the Brown children pick berries.

The swallows swoop in and out of the barn. Some nest on
old hanging tractor seats. If a baby bird tumbles from its
nest, Mrs. Brown gently returns it.

In the driveway, an antique crop duster sits on a flatbed
truck. It looks like a mechanical octopus and will soon join
Farmer Brown's collection of farm equipment.

One of the pigs likes to explore the farm wearing a harness.

In a far field, the donkeys roll in the dust to escape the
flies.

Summer is edging into fall. Apples are growing heavy on the trees. The Browns pick and load them onto the pickup truck. They divide the apples into three groups: bruised for pigs, slightly bruised for cider, and perfect for customers.

In the next field, pumpkins, squash, and gourds are fat and ripe. Farmer Brown will load his prize pumpkin onto the truck, ready to carry to the County Fair.

The barn porch is overflowing with fall fruits and vegetables including tomatoes, squash, peppers, apples, cabbage, and corn. Tiny orange and "baby boo" pumpkins line the windowsills. Wagons and wheelbarrows are filled with hay and pumpkins. The days are shorter, the nights cooler.

Soon the frosts will come and the farm will slow to its
winter rest. But the little farm by the sea never really sleeps.